For Hannah and Joni Macaroni

First published 2005 by Macmillan Children's Books
This edition published 2006 by Macmillan Children's Books
A division of Macmillan Publishers Limited
20 New Wharf Road, London N1 9RR
Basingstoke and Oxford
Associated companies throughout the world
www.panmacmillan.com

ISBN-13: 978-1-4050-5503-1
ISBN-10: 1-4050-5503-1

3 5 7 9 8 6 4 2

A CIP catalogue record for this book is available from the British Library.

Printed in Belgium by Proost.

Mabel's Magical Garden

Paula Metcalf

MACMILLAN CHILDREN'S BOOKS

Mabel's garden
was full of flowers.
They gleamed in
the sunshine.

Every day Nigel and George came to
admire them. "I wish we had such beautiful
flowers in our garden," said George.

"They look like
pretty jewels,"
said Nigel.

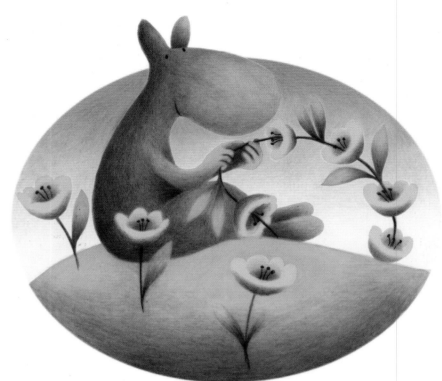

"They smell
like perfume,"
said George.

Sometimes Mabel's friends stayed all day.
They had such fun, they didn't want to go home.

But one morning George and Nigel didn't come.
Mabel waited . . . and then she went to look for them.
She found them busy watering their own garden.

"Look!" called George. "Look at our lovely flowers!"
Mabel frowned. "They're not *your* flowers," she said,
"they're *mine*. You must have stolen them in the night!"
"We didn't steal them," said Nigel.
"They just appeared!" said George.

But Mabel didn't believe them.

That night Mabel
didn't get a wink of sleep.
She was too worried
about somebody
stealing her flowers.

So the next day she built a high wall
all the way round her garden.

It was too high for Nigel to jump over, and too high for
George to reach over (even on tiptoes).

But it was also too high for something else to get in.
Something very important for flowers . . .

. . .the sun.

Without sunshine, the flowers didn't look like pretty jewels and they didn't smell like perfume.

Mabel watered them.

She sang to them.

She even danced for them.

But nothing worked.
"Please get better," she whispered.

Inside the wall, Mabel and her
flowers grew sadder and sadder.

Outside the wall, something wonderful had happened. Nigel and George wanted to share the wonderful thing with Mabel, but the wall was too high for them.

But it was not too high for the little bird.
He flew up and perched on the top.

"Mabel!" he called. "Come and see!"

She put a ladder against
the wall and began to climb.
When she got to the top,
Mabel couldn't believe
what she saw . . .

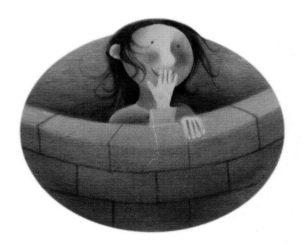

...thousands of flowers ~ everywhere!

"They're so beautiful!" gasped Mabel. "But where did they come from?"

Nobody knew.

Just then there was a huge gust of wind.

"Look everyone!" called Nigel.

"Look at the seeds flying!"

Mabel started to laugh. "So that's how
the flowers have been spreading!"
"Yes," said George, "and if we take the wall
down they'll spread into your garden too!"

Brick by brick, they took down the wall.

When the hard work was
done, everybody sat down for
a rest in the warm sun.

"Aren't we lucky to have such lovely flowers," sighed Nigel. "Yes, and to have each other to share them with," said Mabel.

"I'm sorry I thought you had stolen my flowers."

Then, to show how sorry she was,
Mabel made the most delicious picnic Nigel and
George had ever tasted. And as the sun went
down, everyone admired the beautiful flowers . . .

...together.